MAKEDA

QUEEN OF SHEBA

MAKEDA
QUEEN OF SHEBA

Ronald Harrill

illustrations by
Daryl Shon Anderson

James C. Winston
Publishing Company, Inc.

Trade Division of Winston-Derek Publishers Group, Inc.

PUBLISHED BY JAMES C. WINSTON PUBLISHING COMPANY, INC.
Nashville, Tennessee 37205

Library of Congress Catalog Card No: 93-60916
ISBN: 1-55523-651-0

Printed in the United States of America

To Denise, Kenyon, Aaron, and Nathan;
to the mighty Ethiopians;
and to the ancient writers of the Kebra Nagast.

At the age of twelve, Makeda knew that she would become queen of one of the greatest empires in the world.

She was the only child of the king and queen of Ethiopia. Her country was located on the east coast of Africa, south of Egypt. In ancient times before the birth of Christ, their empire also included the countries of Arabia, Sudan, and Yemen. The empire's army was so large and powerful that few countries dared to cross into their borders.

Makeda knew the title of queen would require a lifetime of service to her country and people. Her father was growing quite old and soon would be unable to carry out the duties of king.

One warm summer morning, Makeda decided to walk to a nearby forest and think about her future. Her dark eyes twinkled as she skipped merrily out into the courtyard.

Such a lovely day, she thought, as she inhaled the freshness of the air. The sweet smell of blooming flowers and fruit trees was everywhere.

The dark brown goatskin sandals she wore matched the color of her smooth brown skin. The bright yellow and blue colors in her robe matched the yellow flower in her black hair.

She decided to gather some flowers to place around her father's throne. Remembering a garden where beautiful flowers grew, she began to run along the edges of the forest. Soon she had gone so far that she was barely able to see the palace.

Stopping to rest for a moment, Makeda was frightened by a loud rustling noise in some nearby bushes. The noise grew louder and moved closer with each passing moment.

Could it be a wild goat? she thought. Or one of the pet animals that lives along the gates of the palace?

Suddenly, to her horror, a full grown male jackal sprang from the bushes. It stared wildly at her, baring its large, ferocious teeth.

Makeda screamed with all her might, hoping to frighten the jackal away or to alert someone nearby. Her skin was hot from fear. She thought her life might come to an end.

As the animal moved closer to the frightened princess, Makeda noticed that its body was covered with fighting scars and that it was limping slightly. She realized that she must fight to save her life, or she would be at the mercy of the beast.

She spied a large stick laying on the ground to her left and quickly moved to grab it.

Her sudden movement was met by a loud snarl and a powerful lunge from the jackal. Just as Makeda's hand reached the stick, she felt a piercing pain in her leg, a pain so great that she screamed louder than before.

She looked down and saw that the jackal had bitten deeply into her foot and ankle. Blood was pouring from the wound, and the pain continued to increase. Sweat was dripping from her face and hands as she raised the stick high in the air. I can't let it kill me, she thought. I must fight back!

With a surge of energy, Makeda struck the jackal squarely on the ear with her weapon. The sudden jolt caused the animal to loosen its grip on her injured foot.

Before the beast could recover, Makeda delivered another blow to his head. She continued to strike the animal even though her leg was throbbing in pain.

Soon the jackal stopped moving. By then, Makeda had grown weak. She sat down to take a close look at her injuries. The skin on her ankle was torn and bleeding.

"Oh no!" she cried. "I can't move my foot. Someone please help me! Help me please!"

Just then, two farmers emerged from the forest. They had heard her cries while tending to their crops and rushed over to help.

They found the princess still clutching the stick. Her beautiful robe was covered with blood.

"Come," said one of the farmers, "we must take you to our village."

"No," said Makeda, "I am the daughter of the king. Take me to the royal palace, and please hurry." At her request, the two men lifted the wounded girl and ran along the path that led to the palace.

When they reached the gates and called out to the guards, the princess was barely awake. Her body was limp, and her eyes were closed as if she were in a deep sleep.

"Hurry!" said the guards. "Bring her inside. You there," he said to another soldier, "go tell the king and the doctors."

"Come, my friend," said one farmer to the other. "Let's take the girl inside and lay her down."

Within minutes, the king and queen were by Makeda's side. The queen began to cry as she gazed upon her injured daughter.

"What happened?" demanded the king. "Tell me what or who caused these injuries to my daughter!"

The farmers told the king of Makeda's screams and how they came to the princess's rescue. "We brought her here as quickly as we could. We hope we did the correct thing, dear king."

"You did, my faithful people, and I am very thankful for your deed."

"Dear king," said the farmer, "you have a very brave daughter. She saved her own life by destroying the jackal. Without her courage, she would have surely died. We hope that she lives a long life, because she will grow to become a great queen. Our kingdom will be blessed to have her lead us. We will pray for her full recovery."

The queen reached down to touch her daughter's face. She watched the doctors carefully tend Makeda's wounds.

"How is she?" asked the queen.

"She is hurt badly," replied the doctor, "and will require plenty of rest. Luckily, the animal missed her major ankle bone, but the bites are very deep. She will recover from the injuries, but she will have a slight limp until she grows older. Some scars will always remain, but she will have a normal life."

"Thank you, doctor, and thanks to all of you," said the king with relief. "We are happy that she will survive this terrible accident."

At last the doctors left, and Makeda's parents were alone with their sleeping daughter. "My husband," said the queen, "our daughter is indeed very brave. I believe that she will grow to become a great leader of our people."

❦

The princess rested in bed for several weeks after her ordeal. She had maids and doctors to help her, and her leg and foot were kept in clean bandages at all times.

One month passed before she felt strong enough to take small steps on her healing foot. At first the pain was great, but with each day she was able to walk better.

After two months, Makeda began a normal schedule of activities. But each night, she continued to bathe her injured foot. The scars constantly reminded her of the battle with the wild animal.

Years later, as her fifteenth birthday approached, Makeda had grown quite tall and beautiful. She was taller than most females in the kingdom, and she seemed very proud of her height. Her long arms and legs were like those of the runners that competed in the athletic games each year.

Lately, she had begun to notice a weary look on her father's face. He seemed to be growing old and tired. She knew that he had worked hard to be a good king for the country.

One day as Makeda was sitting alone in the courtyard, her mother approached her and sat down for a talk. Makeda was feeding fresh fruit to some small birds, who were joyously flying around to pluck the food from her hand. The sun was brightly glowing through the trees.

"My daughter," said Queen Ismenie, "I have been waiting for the proper time to talk with you about your future. I have constantly prayed that you will develop into a good leader of our people.

"You have been blessed with good physical strength, wisdom, and courage. It is your rightful place to become queen of the Ethiopian empire. A queen must be patient and understanding.

She must be fair and honest towards all people. A queen must be brave and honorable at all times.

"My precious daughter, you have all of these noble qualities. You are still quite young, but do not be afraid. Our ancestors will guide you along the right paths of life.

"Our ancestors were great African people. Long before Egypt became a powerful nation, the Ethiopians ruled our land and many of the nearby countries. Our ancestors will guide you as you grow wise and powerful."

Later that evening, all alone in her room, Makeda prayed to her ancestors. She asked for the wisdom and courage needed to become a good queen. Her mother's words inspired her to try to become the best queen that she could for her people.

Two months later, the official news that the king had died spread throughout the land. The people were saddened by his loss and cried openly throughout the ceremonies held to honor the king.

One evening, Queen Ismenie called for Makeda to visit her room for a private talk. "My daughter," she said, "our hearts are sad with grief. But we must begin preparations for your crowning as the new queen. Go now, my daughter, and return to your room for a restful night."

All that night, Makeda lay awake in her bed and looked at the stars. She could not sleep with so many things to think about. Becoming queen is such an honor, she thought to herself.

"How will I learn all of the things required of me? How will I ensure that everyone is treated fairly? The children will need to be well fed and feel safe in our land. How will I watch over them at all times? And what if our country is attacked by enemies? Will my army properly defend our land?"

The heavenly stars seemed to brighten with each soft teardrop that fell from her sparkling eyes. But on that night, Makeda promised herself that she would become a great and caring queen.

One week later, Makeda was crowned the queen of the Ethiopian empire. She was fifteen years old and just growing into womanhood. The date was 1005 years before the birth of Christ.

At Makeda's coronation, the army was present with thousands of soldiers. There were musicians playing beautiful tunes that filled the air with harmony. People from many parts of the kingdom had journeyed great distances to see their new queen for the first time.

Makeda was dressed in a magnificent purple robe trimmed with gold threads. She wore a shining crown adorned with precious stones.

Standing very tall and beautiful, she was the perfect symbol of a queen. As she gazed upon the cheering people, she remembered her promise to become a great leader.

During Makeda's early years as queen, the empire continued to grow and prosper. She received training and education from the teachers in the palace. She listened with enthusiasm as the wise elders told her about the history of the empire.

The people quickly accepted Makeda as the new ruler. She shared the wealth of the country with the people, giving them gold and silver when they needed money, and this made them very happy. She worked hard to make sure that the children were healthy and had food to eat.

The kingdom was blessed with plenty of natural treasures. Some of the greatest riches in the empire came from the southern part of Arabia known as Sheba.

There were plenty of gold mines and emerald sites that produced precious stones. Along the Red Sea were a large number of pearl beds, and the pearls from those beds became the prized

possessions of very wealthy people. Sapphires and beautiful topaz stones were gathered and sold to countries for large sums of money. Spices and perfume plants were also found in many parts of the land.

All of these items brought great wealth and fame to the Ethiopians. People in nearby and faraway countries would pay great prices to have the precious items.

During her fifth year as queen, Makeda received a message that Tamrin, chief of the merchant ships for the empire, wanted to speak with her. Tamrin was a businessman and traveler, and he carried gold, precious stones, incense, perfumes, and fine wood to neighboring countries to sell. Tamrin possessed a good reputation for honesty in both Egypt and Jerusalem. In fact, his loyalty and honesty were so remarkable that Makeda appointed him commander of three hundred ships and many camel caravans for his business duties.

Upon learning of his request to meet with her, Makeda knew that he must have very important matters to discuss. She instructed a soldier to tell Tamrin to come to the royal palace.

Soon Tamrin appeared before her and asked permission to speak. "My queen," he said to her, "I offer you this report on my latest visit to Jerusalem.

"I was able to deliver and sell all of the goods in Jerusalem. King Solomon, leader of the Hebrew people, paid us very high prices for the fine wood. He plans to use the wood to build temples in his kingdom. He even asked that we deliver more precious wood and perfumes to him as soon as we can supply them. And as a sign of friendship and respect for our people, he also offered us good places to sleep and eat.

"During my visit, I realized that he has remarkable wisdom, understanding and love for his people. His knowledge of government matters and fair treatment of people were wonderful to watch. He helped his workers draw the building plans for the magnificent temples. He also taught the men how to place the stones in perfect shapes for the walls.

"There are no human deeds that this king cannot perform. His wisdom is greater than that of any man I have ever met.

"He and his people worship only one God. They believe their God is the supreme ruler of all people. This is why I wanted you to know about this man called Solomon."

Makeda thought carefully about the stories she had just heard. Smiling, she said, "Thank you, dear Tamrin, for your report. I will think about King Solomon, and I will talk with you soon."

For several days, Makeda thought about the king and the people of Jerusalem. Then she called for Tamrin to meet with her at the palace.

"Tamrin, I have given your report careful thought. If King Solomon is as wise as you say, then I would like to visit his country.

"I know that wisdom and knowledge are great treasures to have if you are the leader of a country. I believe that wisdom is more precious than gold or silver. If Solomon is the wisest of all rulers, then I shall visit and learn from this king. How far away is Jerusalem from our country?"

"My queen," answered Tamrin, "Jerusalem is a city located to the north at a great distance from us. We would travel mostly through the desert areas, where the sun would be extremely hot during the day. We also might see violent sand storms. The trip would be a long and tiring one for you to make. I do not think any queen has ever made such a difficult journey as this one. But it would not be all bad, for we would make stops along the way at small villages to receive proper rest and food. I can assure you that the villagers will welcome you with much joy and celebration."

"And Tamrin," asked Makeda, "how long will it take to reach Jerusalem?"

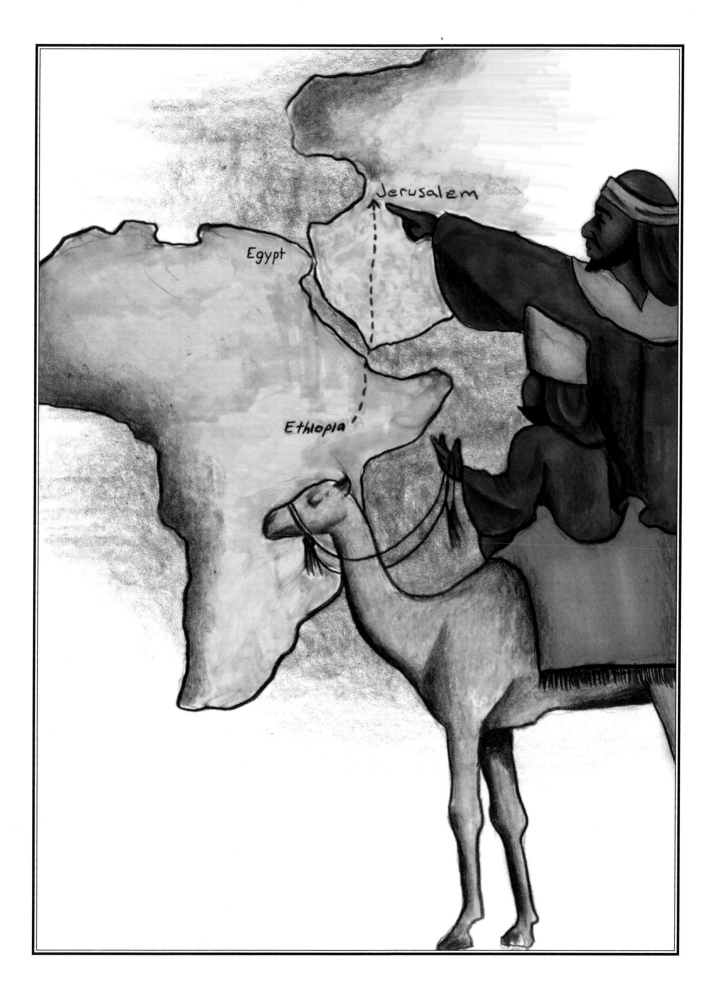

"With a full caravan of camels, supplies, and people, we can make the journey in nine months."

"Then go, Tamrin, and prepare for the journey. I will tell the generals of the army to prepare enough men for the trip. I want you to also prepare a large gift of gold, precious stones, and perfumes for King Solomon."

The news of the journey spread quickly among Makeda's people. Some were glad to hear of the journey, while others were very afraid for their queen.

During the lengthy and complex preparations for the trip, Makeda held many discussions with her people. In particular, as the departure day grew near, one group of loyal servants asked to speak with her in private. Makeda quickly granted their request.

"Dear queen," said one, "you are truly a wise leader. You are intelligent, fair, and honest with all people. No one in the kingdom has ever said that you were not a wise leader. Tell us, queen, why do you want to make such a dangerous journey?"

Makeda graciously responded, "Education and knowledge are the most important things that I could ever obtain. Yes, I am queen and very rich in treasures. But education is more valuable than silver or gold, and knowledge is the greatest of all treasures.

"My heart and mind want to be filled with knowledge. A person that has knowledge is richer than the person who has only money, for wealth alone does not make a person wise.

"In Jerusalem, I will study with some of the greatest teachers in the world. I will learn as much as they are able to teach, and I will grow in wisdom. The journey will indeed be long and difficult for everyone. But my life will not be complete if I miss the chance to learn from the great teachers and from King Solomon."

"Dear queen," said the elder member of the group, "it is our desire to travel with you and protect you during this journey to Jerusalem. We know that you face a difficult journey ahead, and we all wish to be with you, whether in life or in death."

"Thank you my people," replied Makeda, "for you have touched my heart with your loyalty and kindness. I will tell Tamrin to arrange for you to travel with me."

Soon the departure day arrived and the travelers began to assemble in the courtyard. The army, servants, and animals were gathered together under the watchful eyes of Tamrin. Some of the travelers brought their families along to say goodbye, and there was much hugging and crying as relatives said their last words to each other.

The day was sunny and noisy as people moved quickly to gather their supplies. Seven hundred and ninety-seven camels took their place in the caravan, and hundreds of donkeys went behind the camels. All the animals were loaded with supplies, including the treasures for King Solomon.

Tamrin then led the queen to a special camel that carried a lambskin saddle and an umbrella for protection from the sun. Makeda was dressed in a long white robe that would help keep her cool in the heat of the sun. As she took her place in the group, her people gathered in large numbers to bid her farewell. They said a special prayer asking the ancestors to protect the queen and the caravan from harm. Then the group was at last ready to leave their homeland and head north towards Jerusalem.

Day after day, the caravan marched through the desert. Sometimes the temperature reached 115 degrees during the day. Other days, the desert storms would blow sand so hard

that the caravan was forced to find shelter until the winds calmed down. But under the careful direction of Tamrin, the group was still able to travel at a good speed.

Villagers living throughout the desert welcomed the travelers and sheltered them for many nights. For many, this was the first opportunity to meet and talk with the queen, and they were amazed at her beauty and wisdom. Her face was as beautiful as any woman's they had seen, her dark brown skin was smooth and flawless, and her tall stature made her seem like a special kind of person.

During these visits, Makeda talked with the people and answered all of their questions. And before leaving each village, she met privately with the women and young girls. She encouraged them to be the best mothers and guardians of the Ethiopian people they could be.

For months, the group continued to travel from village to village, always moving closer to Jerusalem. The news of the queen's presence continued to spread throughout all regions of the desert until the villages became a blanket of protection and safe passage for the queen.

After eight months of travel, the caravan approached the borders of Jerusalem. When Makeda looked around, she saw miles of green plants and flowers thriving in the rich and fertile soil surrounding the city.

When they finally neared the end of their journey, Tamrin selected five men to travel to Jerusalem and announce the coming of the queen. To ensure their safety, he asked some Hebrew shepherd men to travel with them.

When the men arrived at the entrance to Jerusalem, they were met by soldiers. The leader of the Ethiopians spoke first. "Greetings, our friends! We have come to deliver a message to King Solomon. It is with great honor that we announce that Makeda, Queen of the Ethiopian empire, has journeyed to Jerusalem. She has come to visit with your great and wise king. Our queen is only a short journey behind us, awaiting your welcome."

"Come with us," replied a soldier. "We will take you to the royal palace. We have heard wonderful stories of your great queen, and our king will be pleased to hear of her arrival."

Together, the group marched to the palace, where they found the king attending to government matters. The leader of the Hebrew soldiers greeted the king and was given permission to speak.

"My king," he said, "these men are Ethiopian, and they wish to give you a message from their queen."

Solomon then spoke. "Greetings, dear brothers. In the name of our God, I welcome you to our land. Please tell me the message that you bring from your honored queen."

The Ethiopian spokesman answered, "King Solomon, Queen Makeda, ruler of all Ethiopians, brings you greetings from our people. She has traveled to your land and wishes to enter Jerusalem."

"Yes," replied Solomon, "I have received reports that your caravan was approaching Jerusalem. I understand that you are being led by the most respected of merchants, Tamrin. It is with great pleasure that I receive the news of your queen's arrival.

"Jerusalem welcomes your queen and people with open arms. Preparations will be made to celebrate this occasion. Please go and tell the queen that I welcome her in the name of our God. I will be waiting patiently for her arrival. Please give my dear friend Tamrin my best wishes."

The men left the palace to report to the queen. When they arrived, Makeda, Tamrin, and the others listened eagerly to the description of their visit.

"We arrived in Jerusalem and were treated most graciously by King Solomon and his people. The king awaits your visit. He

also sends his best wishes to Tamrin. Anything that we need will be provided by the people of the palace."

With a gleam in his eyes and a confident smile, Tamrin instructed the group to prepare for the final miles to Jerusalem. There was much singing and joy among the Ethiopians as they gathered for the final march. The servants busily attended to the supplies and the animals, and the soldiers laughed and joked as they gathered their weapons and clothing.

The next morning, the caravan marched toward the city with loud and joyous singing that could be heard for miles around. The villagers of Jerusalem stood along the roads and watched in amazement as the caravan moved closer to the city.

On the last night of the journey, there were ceremonies and celebrations long past the midnight hour. As the sun began to rise the next morning, they awoke and prepared to enter Jerusalem.

Makeda herself was awakened by her servants, who carried fresh water for her bath. Next came a servant who brought the royal robe, jewelry, and crown that were worn on special occasions.

Makeda first dressed in the long, flowing, dark purple robe that was trimmed in pure gold stitching and had rubies and other precious stones neatly sewn around the shoulders. As she dressed, she thought about King Solomon. She wondered how he would greet her and the people of her empire. Then she put on the jewelry that had been made just for her. She looked at the beautiful gold earrings with the dangling sapphire stones, and her fingers traced the lines of the gold and ruby bracelets that she would wear on each wrist. Around her neck she would wear a necklace of pearls, diamonds, and topaz stones. And still, she thought about the people of this new land and how they would accept her.

Suddenly, she was roused from her daydreams by the faithful Tamrin. He was standing by the doorway of her tent asking permission to enter.

"Please come in," said Makeda.

Tamrin entered and spoke. "My queen, it is time to enter the city of Jerusalem. King Solomon has sent some of his soldiers to escort us. With your permission, we will make our plans."

"You may proceed with your duties," replied the queen.

Finally the group approached the main gates. They were greeted by a band of flute players and drummers, all of whom marched along to honor the coming of the queen. The people living near the palace stood along the road and cheered the queen as she passed by. Fathers proudly held their children high in the air so they could get a glimpse of her. Makeda looked like a goddess dressed in the finest robe and jewelry that they had ever seen. She smiled to the people and stretched out her arms with love to the children.

Soon she stood before the city gates. The caravan stopped at the entrance, and hundreds of soldiers came forth and bowed humbly before her. At this, there was more cheering and clapping as people stood on hilltops and buildings to see the queen.

"They are delighted to see you," said Tamrin. "The people know your good deeds and reputation. Now, my queen, we will go directly to the main palace where King Solomon and the royal court await you."

Tamrin and a leader of the Hebrew army moved to the front of the group. Together, they took the others onto a wide avenue leading to the palace.

After a few minutes, the group came to a stop. The queen was escorted down from her seat, and she stood before the great temple built by Solomon.

There were guards, musicians, storytellers, and magicians all gathered for the occasion, but suddenly the music stopped and all eyes turned to the large temple doors. They swung open, and King Solomon emerged.

The queen studied the famous ruler and thought that he appeared just as Tamrin had described him. He was tall, with broad shoulders and a very handsome face, and his legs and arms were muscular like those of an athlete. His eyes were dark, and they sparkled with the daylight. He is, she thought to herself, certainly the picture of a king.

As he moved towards her, she wondered about him. Was he as kind, humble, and wise as he was in the stories she had heard?

Then Solomon spoke. "Queen Makeda, ruler of all Ethiopians, your wisdom and courage are known throughout the world. You are the greatest of all queens. You are both beautiful and wise, and I welcome you to Jerusalem. This is the land of the Hebrew people. We are servants of the one God of all people.

"We are delighted to have you in our country. Your every wish will be granted by my servants. Your soldiers, servants, and animals will be treated with great care."

The queen looked directly at King Solomon and replied, "I accept your welcome, great king of the Hebrew people. I bring you greetings from the people of Ethiopia. We have traveled a

great distance to visit you. Your good reputation is known throughout the world, and we are delighted to be among your people."

"Come," said Solomon, "my servants have prepared our guest quarters for you. You will be able to rest after your long journey. Tonight, we will have a banquet in your honor.

"Tamrin, please inform my servants of everything that you need for your soldiers and the others. Your people will be given full sleeping areas and will eat the best foods that we have to offer." After these words, the queen and her special maids were escorted to her guest quarters.

On the first evening, the city was filled with singing and dancing. The queen and her court were taken to the royal banquet room for a special meal of the finest meats, vegetables, and fruits. Two special chairs were built for the king and visiting queen. Together, they watched as musicians played and danced well into the night. When the ceremonies and dining had ended, the queen returned to her guest quarters.

After several days of rest, the queen was ready to begin her meetings with the king. On the morning of the first meeting, Makeda was escorted to the palace where Solomon awaited her. After greeting her, he asked that she begin her questions.

"King Solomon," she began, "I have heard many stories about your wisdom, knowledge, and understanding of all things in the world. Tell me, king, how did you become so wise?"

"Great queen, I am not the one who is wise and all knowing. It is the God of Israel, whom I must serve, that deserves all credit and praise. Our God is just and fair. He guides me in the daily matters of my life, and he has given me the talents I have. Without the guidance of God, I would not have this wisdom and understanding. All things come from God, and I am merely his faithful servant."

"Then tell me," Makeda continued, "how does a person receive wisdom and knowledge from your God?"

Solomon answered, "You must believe and trust completely in God. And you must follow in the worship and faith as set forth in His holy commandments.

"I will call upon our priests and teachers to talk with you about our God and our religion. The priests will answer all of your questions. I too, will continue to share wisdom with you on this and other matters."

The queen had many meetings with the priests and with Solomon to discuss religion and government. Soon she began to understand more about the God of Israel.

Each day, Makeda observed Solomon's leadership skills as he ruled on all affairs of the land. Concerning government matters, building projects, and the problems of the people, he seemed to always find the correct solutions. She was amazed at the wisdom of this one man. His deeds were remarkable in her eyes.

Makeda learned that people came from many cities and countries to hear Solomon speak. They asked him questions about God, science, mathematics, and history, and Solomon answered all their questions with the wisdom that came from God. He did not brag about his knowledge but was always humble when talking with his people. And he always thanked God for enabling him to teach people about the world.

As time went by, Makeda learned more and more about the world. Yet the more she learned, the more her curiosity grew. During one private meeting with Solomon, Makeda decided to discuss religion with him once more.

"My people worship the sun," she began. "The sun provides us with warmth and daylight. Our ancestors also worshiped the the sun. Tell me, Solomon, if I did not worship the sun, then whom should I worship?"

"Our God created the sun, stars, and everything in the world," replied Solomon. "It is because of God that the sun provides you with warmth and sunshine.

"God created man and woman. He created the ocean and all things that live in its waters. He has given us all the things we have. We should be thankful to God for everything."

Then Makeda replied, "I will worship your God as my own God, because this seems right to me. It is because of your God that I was able to travel safely to Jerusalem, and I have been blessed to come here and learn about the true God of the world. King Solomon, what I now know of God is the greatest thing I could have learned from you."

The time came when the queen had been in Jerusalem for over six months, and she decided that it was time to return to her own country. During Tamrin's next visit with her, she told him of her wishes to return home.

"My queen," said Tamrin, "with the blessings of King Solomon, I will make preparations for the journey. I will inform our soldiers of your wishes."

"Thank you, Tamrin," Makeda said. "I myself will inform the king tonight of my plans."

That evening, Solomon's heart was saddened with her news. He asked the queen to stay longer so that she could learn more about God.

At his request, the queen thanked him for his kindness, and she decided to stay in Jerusalem for another month to complete her studies.

A month later, travel plans were finally made for the return trip. Solomon made certain that the Ethiopians were given all of the supplies that they needed for their journey.

On the evening before their departure, Queen Makeda met with King Solomon for the last time. "Solomon," she said, "your wisdom and knowledge are as great as that of any man I have met. You have taught me many wonderful things about the God of Israel and the religion of your people. I am grateful for the generosity you have shown my people. In return, I wish you eternal happiness and peace."

Solomon smiled and replied, "Makeda, we have learned many things from you and your people as well. The mighty Ethiopian empire is blessed to have such a wise and loving queen. We will pray to our God to protect you on your journey."

The next morning, Makeda and her servants gathered at the palace to bid farewell to the people. King Solomon and his

court were all present to say goodbye to the visitors. The courtyard was full of people who wanted to get one last look at the Queen of Ethiopia.

After bidding farewell to Solomon, Makeda stepped forward onto the balcony and waved to the cheering crowd. Then she and her people departed for their homeland. They carried with them the treasures and supplies that were gifts from the people of Jerusalem.

They traveled again through the desert and stopped at many of the same villages they had visited before. The people were pleased to see that the queen was alive and on her way home. After nine months, they finally reached the gates of their kingdom. Over two years had passed since the queen had left her homeland.

When the caravan arrived in Ethiopia, the people honored Makeda with a grand celebration. The priests, military officers, and officials greeted her with gifts honoring her return. The crowd cheered joyfully for hours at the return of their beloved queen. Makeda waved to the happy people and received hugs and kisses from those around her. Then the caravan, followed by the cheering people, marched to the royal palace.

Once they reached the palace, Makeda stood on the steps as the soldiers brought forth the gifts from Jerusalem. She gave gold and silver to her faithful court members, who had stayed at home while she traveled. She gave many of the women beautiful robes and clothes she had received in Jerusalem. Before long, she had given away most of the treasures to the people of her kingdom.

The celebrations honoring the queen's return continued for several weeks while Makeda surveyed her kingdom. She was pleased that the leaders had taken such good care of the people while she was away. Her heart was filled with joy, and she decided to give an official speech telling the people about her long journey.

When the day of her speech arrived, Makeda said, "My people, I have completed my mission to travel to the land of King Solomon. It was there that I received lessons from the great teachers. I am glad of the knowledge and wisdom that I received in Jerusalem. I studied and listened with care as the teachers spoke to me.

"I often thought of our people while I was away. Yes, I have returned to you a much wiser queen. I pray that I will always be able to lead our people in the ways of peace and love."

For many years to come, the empire continued to grow under the careful leadership of Makeda. She taught her people about God and how He was responsible for all things in the world.

And so was born the legend of Queen Makeda, who ruled over Ethiopia for fifty years. When she died near the age of sixty-five, her fame and fortune were known all over the world.

In Israel, the people continued to talk about the great queen who came from the south. Hebrew parents told their children stories about Makeda for many years. Even the Bible tells her story, in the book of First Kings, Chapter 10: "And when the Queen of Sheba heard of the fame of Solomon concerning the name of the Lord, she came to prove him with hard questions. And she came to Jerusalem with a very great train, with camels that bore spices, and very much gold, and precious stones."

The stories of Makeda were passed down through history and were part of the early teaching of the young child, Jesus. And as a grown man, one thousand years after Makeda's death, Jesus spoke of the great queen from Ethiopia in Matthew, Chapter 12, verse 42: "The queen of the South shall rise up in judgment with this generation, for she came from the uttermost part of the earth to hear the wisdom of Solomon."

Such is the story of Makeda, beloved Queen of Ethiopia. Unto her was given wisdom, glory, riches, and everlasting fame.